CTW SESAME STREET

Happy and Sad, Grouchy and Glad

By Constance Allen
Illustrated by Tom Brannon

A SESAME STREET/GOLDEN PRESS BOOK
Published by Western Publishing Company, Inc.,
in conjunction with Children's Television Workshop.

This educational book was created in cooperation with the Children's Television Workshop, producers of SESAME STREET. Children do not have to watch the television show to benefit from this book. Workshop revenues from this product will be used to help support CTW educational projects.

Oh welcome, oh welcome to our little play.
We are ever so glad you could join us today!
We are going to talk about FEELINGS! And so,
please open the curtain and on with the show!

We are two furry monsters,
one red and one blue.
We can count up to twenty
and tie our own shoe.
We can sing oh-so-sweetly—
OR SHOUT VERY LOUD!
Have you guessed how we feel?
We're both feeling PROUD!

Here's a big plate of cookies
all gooey and sweet—
with big chocolate chips!
What time do we eat?

When me have some cookies,
that make me feel GLAD!

But when the plate's empty...
  (Hmm. Maybe just one or two
  to see how they taste.
  Mmmm! Delicious!
  Gobble, gobble!)
me feel very SAD!

To show you *my* feeling
I'll do a short dance.

I am feeling EMBARRASSED
in polka-dot pants!

When Oscar's up late
and makes too much noise,
when people at play group
will not share their toys,
when my birdseed pancakes
turn out to be lumpy,
I sit in a corner
and feel really GRUMPY!

Pizza and ice cream,
my little pet fish,
my warm fuzzy blankie,
my favorite dish,
cute furry kitties,
and honey on toast—
these things are nice,
but I LOVE Mommy most!

Mumford's my name.
Many tricks I perform.
I pull rabbits from hats.
I can make a rainstorm!

A LA PEANUT BUTTER
SANDWICHES!

Good heavens, my rabbits
are extra-large-sized!
It's snowing, not raining—
even I feel SURPRISED!

I'm Shelley the Turtle.
I'll make my rhyme brief,
for I'm shaking and trembling
up here like a leaf!
I feel awfully SHY,
in case you can't tell,
so if nobody minds
I'll go back in my shell.

When your crayons get broken,
you've lost your new shoe,
your picnic gets rained on,
you've nothing to do,
you stub your big toe,
and you have to yell OUCH!
Well, then, what could be better?
You feel like a GROUCH!

I *do* not like thunder and lightning, do you?
Or little white ghosts that creep up and shout, "BOO!"
Or tigers that growl and look underfed!
These make me so SCARED, I crawl under my bed!

When we're feeling HAPPY,
we stand on our heads
and we dance all around
and we jump on our beds!
We sing tra-la-la
and we laugh ho-ho-ho!
When we're feeling HAPPY,
we let the world know!

And that is the ending of our little play.
We thank you for sharing our feelings today!